I AM THE DOG

I AM THE CAT

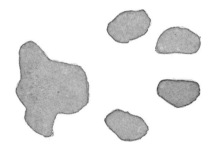

Donald Hall

I AM THE
DOG

I AM THE
CAT

Pictures by Barry Moser

DIAL BOOKS  New York

Published by Dial Books
A member of Penguin Group (USA) Inc.
345 Hudson Street
New York, New York 10014

Designed by Barry Moser
Manufactured in China
First Edition
20 19 18 17 16 15 14

Library of Congress Cataloging in Publication Data
Hall, Donald, 1928–
I am the dog, I am the cat / by Donald Hall ;
pictures by Barry Moser.—1st ed.   p.   cm.
Summary: A dog and a cat take turns explaining what
is wonderful about being who they are.
ISBN 0-8037-1504-8 (trade)
ISBN 0-8037-1505-6 (library)
[1. Dogs—Fiction.   2. Cats—Fiction.]
I. Moser, Barry, ill.   II. Title.
PZ7.H14115Iaac 1994   [E]—dc20   93-28060   CIP   AC

The illustrations were painted with transparent watercolor on paper handmade for the Royal Watercolor
Society by Simon Green. They were then color-separated
and reproduced as red, blue, yellow, and black halftones.

For Ariana and Abigail
D.H.

For Nancy Willard, with love
B.M.

Dog: I am the dog.
I like bones.
I like to *bury* bones.
As for eating, I can take it or leave it—
but I like it when *they* feed me.

CAT: I am the cat.
I don't *care* whether they feed me or not
as long as I get fed.
Sometimes I tease them to feed me,
then turn up my nose at what I get.

Dog: Making the acquaintance of babies,
I allow them to pull my hair.
I do not like it,
but I allow it, for
I am the dog.

Cat: When babies come into the house,
I try to *vanish*.
Babies are crazy!
Babies *sit* on you!

DOG: I am brave as I bark
      to frighten the burglar
      disguised as a U P S man,
      or the kidnapper who pretends to be a
        bicyclist
      wanting a drink of water.

CAT: Strangers are just fine.
      If I feel like a lap, I feel like a lap.
      Why should I care what *they* feel like?

DOG: I sleep all day in order to stay rested,
in order to be alert
when it is my duty to bark.

CAT: I sleep all day
in order to stay awake all night
on mouse patrol.

DOG: After I sleep all day,
I sleep all night, for
I am the dog.

CAT: Cats work hard.
When people and dogs are asleep,
I never stop hunting mice.
In the absence of mice,
I hunt pieces of paper, paper clips, or
rubber bands.

DOG: When I walk in the country, I chase rabbits,
them,
butterflies,
trucks,
and sticks, for
I am the dog.

CAT: When I want to go through a door,
I paw at it and meow.
When they finally open the door,
I don't want to go through it anymore.

DOG: When I smell something wonderful,
I roll in it.

CAT: Every now and then
I decide to act frightened.
From a deep sleep I leap
suddenly into the air,
then run off and hide somewhere.

DOG: I am nervous
when I hear thunder,
firecrackers, or guns,
and nothing *they* say
will comfort me.

CAT: Nothing frightens me.
It's not that I'm brave.
It's just that nothing
frightens me.

DOG: When I walk in town, I sniff at fireplugs,
telephone poles,
fences,
hedges,
and other dogs, for
I am the nose.

CAT: All day long, when I'm awake,
    I watch birds from the top of the
        bread box
    in the pantry window.
    If I listed all the birds I've ever seen,
    the list would go on for a thousand pages.

DOG: I scratch fleas
    suddenly and ferociously.

CAT: Don't touch me! for
    I am the cat.

DOG: When I swim in the pond,
I bark at minnows.
Then I shake water on you, for
I am the dog.

CAT: I keep myself clean.
What if the president dropped by?

DOG: I like chasing a ball.
It amuses me
when *they* beg to get it back.

CAT: The VCR is warm.
It is my bed-in-the-house, for
I am the yawning cat.

DOG: I like my ears scratched.
I like praise.
I cannot bear it when *they* use that tone
of voice.
I am ashamed, for
I am the dog.

CAT: The dog amuses me.
He cares about what people think!
I wash his muzzle.

DOG: I pretend-nip the cat when she washes me.

CAT: Dogs are nervous and well-meaning.
It is well-known that cats
are at the same time
independent,
selfish,
fearless,
beautiful,
cuddly,
scratchy,
and intelligent.

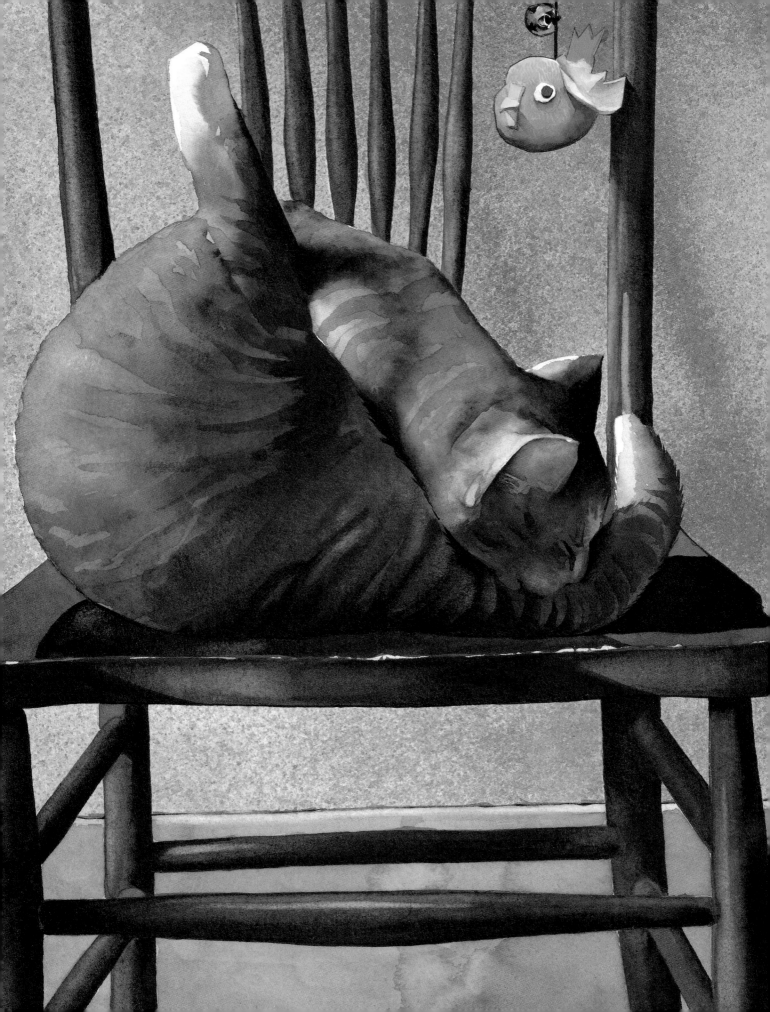

Dog: Cats just don't *care*.
Only a dog
is at the same time
dignified,
guilty,
sprightly,
obedient,
friendly,
vigilant,
and soulful.

CAT: I leap for his throat!
I hurl myself at his muzzle,
which is the same size as I am.
After a while he bows.

DOG: Cats are weird.

CAT: I walk away
with my tail in the air, for
I am the cat.

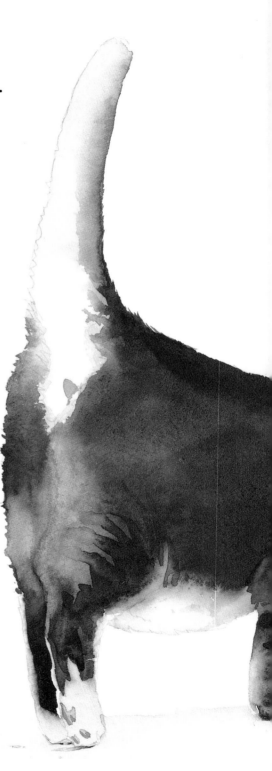